Clint Faraday
book 33
Die Trying

Clint and family are in their little place near Quebrada Tula, on the comarca. He meets and Englishman in the cantina who has a few flakes of gold he found in the river toward the coast. He says he's going to go upriver to find where it came from.

Clint says that area is impenetrable. Only a few of the Indios could survive long in the higher mountains in the area.

The man says he'll find it or die trying.

He dies trying – but from a shot through the heart.

Or does he? Someone did!

Clint Faraday
book 33
Die Trying
© 2019 by C. D. Moulton

This is a work of fiction. Any resemblances to persons, living or dead, or events is purely coincidental unless otherwise stated.

Contents

An Easy Life   pg.   1
English Dan Disappears   pg.   7
C'est la Vie et Mort   pg.   18
Plots and Plans   pg.   34
Eureka! And All That   pg.   42
An E-mail   pg.   59

About the author

CD Moulton has traveled extensively over much of the world both in the music business, where he was a rock guitarist, songwriter and arranger and in an import/export business. He has been everything from a bar owner to auto salvage (junkyard) manager, longshoreman to high steel worker, orchid grower to landscaper, tropical fish farmer to commercial fisherman. He started writing books in 1983 and has published more than 350 books as of January 1, 2023. His most popular books to date are about research with orchids, though much of his science fiction and fantasy work has proven popular. He wrote the CD Grimes, PI series, and the Det. Nick Storie series, Clint Faraday series, and many other works.

He now resides in Gualaca, Chiriqui, Panamá, where he writes books, plays music with friends, does research with orchids and medicinal plants. He has lately become involved in fighting for the rights of the indigenous people, who are among his closest friends, and in fighting the extreme corruption in the courts and police in Panamá.

He offers the free e-book, *Fading Paradise*, that explains what he has been through because of the corruption.

CD is the discoverer of the Chadam Protocol for curing cancer.

Facebook page Ambrosia peruviana for cancer.

Clint Faraday
Die Trying

<u>An Easy Life</u>

Clint Faraday, retired PI from Florida, USA, laid back in his big hammock on the porch of his little cabin in the comarca a short distance from Quebrada Tula and playfully teased his ten month old son, Nito (Clintonito). His beautiful young wife, Tyna, brought him a chicha and climbed into the large hammock to tease both Clint and Nito.

Life here in paradise was easy and pleasant, on the comarca. You didn't fight it, you lived it.

"I think I like this place as much as Cusapín," Clint said. "It's a lot different. Here, we have the mountains and rivers, there, lower mountains and the Caribbean. I think I'll sell the place in Bocas. It's become 'way too much like Key West. Too touristy and too expensive."

"You'll go crazier than you already are. The only murders here are somebody gets mad and chops somebody else apart with a machete. You wouldn't have anything to do!"

"Are you saying I'm crazy, Woman?"

"Sure! I wouldn't have you if you weren't!"

They teased and played awhile more, then Clint said he thought he'd walk into Tula to see what was happening there.

It was a two hour walk. He had the Ducatti, but wanted to live like the friends on the comarca. He might get a horse. He liked to walk. He liked the forest and the few people he met on the way.

He soon headed down the path and along the cool stream that ran from the mountain above his home to near Tula. He talked to four different people going back to their places on the way. The last, just on the outskirts, said there was a really strange man in town. He was asking permission to go into the mountains west and north of Tula. The council chief told him he could go, but there was no responsibility on them. It was bad country, and dangerous.

"He refuses to understand only a fool would go in there if he was from a city. Even we don't go very much," Riko finished.

"It's rainforest jungle. He'd get so lost he'd never find his way out in an hour," Clint agreed. "Why does he want to go in there?"

"He found a little gold in the river below the mountains and a little near here. He says it comes from above and that he wants to find where it comes from. There's that little bit of gold everywhere. Those city people don't have any sense."

"Gold equals money, equals power – to him. I used to believe that, though not so much as a lot of people. Get away from the cities and the stupid ideas of controlling others and you can see how pointless that kind of life is."

They chatted about other things awhile, then Clint went on into the town. He stopped several places to talk with people. He soon ended up in the cantina. The stranger was standing there, arguing with the owner, Arnaldo. Clint knew Naldo and went over to say hello. He was introduced to the stranger.

"Clint, this is English Dan. He wants to go into the higher mountains to look for gold. He can't understand why we say not to go."

"Yes. Daniel Hames Westhampton, Liverpool, England, UK," he replied. "My Spanish isn't very good and a lot of the people out here don't even speak it. I have permission from the chief, here, to go into the mountains, but these people all say I can't. I don't know what's going on!"

"They aren't saying you can't go. They're only advising you not to. It's dangerous for the people who were raised here. For a city person to try it is stupid.

"What's the great need?"

"Here. I found this ore miles back in that stream that runs to the west. I even found some half a kilometer from here! It's coming from higher. I want to find the source!" He handed Clint a plastic packet with about a quarter ounce of gold flakes.

"It's gold. It's in most of the streams around here," Clint said. "You can get about a salary panning it. Most here don't think it's worth the trouble to pan. It doesn't have any particular value unless you go to a city, then you only get money for it. Maybe you can buy some harina or a new machete or boots or something.

"You can go looking for it up there, but it's dangerous. You might find a lode that's a little richer than the washout. You might find a large load, but you aren't going to set up any mine or anything, here. You can take what you can carry, but that's it."

"I've seen that they don't know how much gold can bring them. They don't seem to understand that having that gold will give them everything else they want."

"They don't want things. They have a very good life here without that silliness. You can go after gold if you want, but I'm one who advises against it. You're chasing a fantasy that doesn't even apply, here.

"You're not going into something like this alone, are you?"

"Well, yes, actually. The loner type, don't you know. Adventure and all that, but maybe make a few million pounds doing it."

"Chances of actually finding a large lode are low. Chances of surviving alone in those jungles are lower. Go, if you want. Nobody here is going to stop you. They just feel you're foolish to the point you might actually be crazy. A woman from England said it about right about another thing. 'Rather a nice person, but quite mad, when you consider it.' That's about what they think of you."

He laughed. "And I'd feel forced to agree! I might not find anything, but I'll die trying!"

They chatted about various other philosophical things, then Clint said he had to run a couple of errands, then would walk back home.

"You see? If you had the gold, you could buy a Jeep and drive home!"

"But I have a car in Almirante and a Ducatti here. I could buy anything I want. I'm actually rich, through little fault of my own. What I want in life is here. My wife and son, friends, good food and plentiful, enough clothing to fill actual needs, fresh water and a comfortable home. All the things are what I want and need. More would start to own me, not vice versa.

"Dan, I can walk here and share conversation with a lot of people along the way and enjoy this magnificent scenery. It doesn't cost a thing. I go where I want, when I want, and dress as I want. There are no appointments or schedules and no pressures. I opted out of that life. It's empty. I'm free.

"That's what people don't understand about us Ngobe. We have all those things, but the gringo life is empty. They've given up what's valuable for emptiness."

"You say Ngobe. You're not Indio!"

"Yes, I am. They have made me one of them, to my great honor."

"I meant legally."

"Legally. It was declared by the council. I even have a passport that states I am native Panamanian. All Ngobe are native Panamanians."

"I think I like you. I don't understand you. You're honest, and no one is."

"We all arc, here."

"Well, I wish you bon voyage! I hope to return through here one day soon with all the gold I can carry!"

"I wish you luck. Be careful."

They parted. Clint bought some rice and salt and headed back home.

Clint told Tyna about the strange Englishman. She agreed it was foolish for a single person to try to go into those mountains. They would find him wandering or they would find his dead body up there. There were snakes and poisonous spiders, loose footing up high, and a thousand other dangers to the uninitiated.

He said he wished Dan luck. He was a decent sort of person who was living in a fantasy. He pictured himself as the great adventurer/explorer who spat in death's face. He would charge alone through the dangers, showing the world what he was made of! He would discover the largest and richest lode of gold ever found in the Americas! Thousands of beautiful women would fight for his attention!

Clint grinned and shook his head. He would, if he even survived, find a couple pounds of gold, which would pay for the trip. He would be eaten up by insects. He wouldn't know how much food there was.

The adventure part was partly true, and he had that spirit. The reality was a lot different than the dream.

Life settled into a calm sort of dreamy time for the next two weeks. Clint went into Tula every third or fourth day. Tyna went with him a couple of times, but preferred to stay at the house. She had two neighbors only about a kilometer away. They got along well.

Clint went into Tula the sixteenth day after his first meeting with English Dan to find a woman and two men from Australia there. They were looking for English Dan. Arnaldo introduced Elizabeth "Betty" Ames, Carl Wells and Andrew "Andy" Hopewell, from Perth-Amboy.

"Dan? You mean the strange Englishman?" Clint asked, innocently. Arnaldo had told him in Ngobe that he was suspicious of these people and no one had told them anything except that Dan was there for a couple of days and went off into the jungle.

"Strange! That's Dan!" Betty replied. "He's from Liverpool. My parents were from there. I'm Dan's niece. He ran off – for about the tenth time, I might say – and left his businesses to rot! Carl and Andy are his partners in Australia. Mihael Landsing, the partner from Canada, is out in the jungle somewhere trying to find anyone who saw him anywhere. These people claim they didn't see him, I think. I don't speak much Spanish and they talk in that Indian dialect."

"The ones who go into the cities to sell things and buy things speak Spanish. There's little need of it out here," Clint replied. "If some guy is out there trying to find anyone, he's in for a fairly hard time. Almost none of them speak Spanish."

"Well, Mike does speak Spanish, but not the dialect," Carl said. "He has a knack for finding people, but more in civilized places, if you know what I mean."

"Civilized? I doubt you'd find more civilized people than the Ngobe. It's not the greed-based polluted civilization, if you can call it that, of the cities.

"I met Dan, English Dan, as we called him, for a few minutes. He wanted to find a gold mine or something as silly, but he was really enjoying the adventure. Everyone advised him not to go into those mountains alone. Not many of the natives go in there. It's truly the primeval forest. I give it less than fifty-fifty that he'll return. He's either lost or dead by now."

"You take it that casually that a man might be dead!?" Betty cried.

"What? He was told about the dangers and was advised not to go. He said he'd find the gold or die trying. It's been more than ten days. We can assume that he died trying. It was his choice."

They talked awhile. It seemed that Dan was

already richer than he wanted to be. It was for the fantasy, not the gold itself. He owned controlling interest in several large companies. He hadn't shown for the yearly stockholders' meetings, so they came looking for him.

"What he does, he disappears, all of a sudden. No one knows where he's gone or what he's up to now," Andy explained. "He usually doesn't make it so inopportune a time. He comes back with a new adventure and some kind of trophy. If he's here looking for gold, I can assure you he'll find it. He's phenomenally tenacious and he has a basis for what he does. He'll come back with a twenty pound bag of pure gold nuggets, put them in a case in his study, hang around the businesses for a month or two, then be gone again. We wouldn't much care, except this isn't a good time. Business all over the world is in rather bad shape. We need direction. It wouldn't hurt a lousy thing for the direction to be backed up with his phenomenal luck!"

"Well, he was going to the headwaters of the river a couple of kilometers back. That one joins this one. He found gold fifty or so kilometers farther downstream and more here. That's mean country for experienced people who were born and raised here. He doesn't know what he's in for and he wouldn't listen."

"He'll come marching out of there carrying a sack of gold. He knows what he's doing. He did it in Borneo, in Africa, in Brazil, and he'll do it here," Betty said. "He was looking for something different in each place. He found it in all of them. It's what he is. He won't bow down to nature, but he considers it a friendly sort of competition. He loves nature and it seems to love him back."

"I sensed that in him," Clint said. "We had a very short philosophical conversation. He was able to convince me that he was after the gold because gold is money and power. It didn't seem to fit very well with other parts of his philosophy, but I realize how you can compartmentalize your mind in some ways. You can't know anyone very well in three minutes. Not when you're thinking of other things."

"We wouldn't even bother about it, but this is the wrong time, what with the sorry international business situation," Carl said. "He seems to think the best thing to do is ignore it where we can. Just try to stay head above water until things pick up again. He didn't really seem to think they ever would, but he doesn't much care. He's not in our situation. We have to make this go. It's all we have."

"What kind of business is it?" Clint asked.

"Everything to do with building a house, from

purchasing property to tearing the old one down and building a new one. Financing through selling. All of it. Diversified within the selected game, he calls it," Andy replied. "I'm in the financial end, Betty's in the materials end, Carl's in the labor end and Mike's in the engineering end."

Clint nodded. "Well, I hope he does come out of there with his trophy. I'll be around town most of the day. Maybe we'll meet again. I can see if anyone knows anything about him." He waved and went on to the cantina for some hojaldres and bolitas. Sami was there. He was from the area where Dan had gone. He had talked with him and had said which trail would lead him to the river higher in the mountains.

"The gold is from the Two Deviltree Canyon. There's a lot of it, but it's in a very bad place to try to get any of it out. It will take several days for him to get there."

"You told him that?"

"No. I think he wanted to find it for himself. I only said the river was that way. The gold is down from where the river passes up there. He would be able to find that because there is no gold above."

"Well, we know he got that far."

"Yes. I told the other one he had passed there. He said he would find him. There weren't a lot of places he could be."

"Other one?"

"Yes. The day before yesterday. He was looking for him. He said they were friends in business. Partners."

Clint nodded. That would be Mike.

He went to the almacen and bought some cloth for Tyna. She wanted to make a few things around the house and a couple of the traditional dresses for herself. Orange and green and yellow were her family colors.

He saw Betty just as he was leaving. He told her Dan was seen up in the mountains and Mike was up there looking for him. She thanked him, but seemed nervous. She wouldn't say much of anything more, but his feeling was nervous, not so much worried. Odd!

He was just out of town on his way back home when a gringo came walking toward him on the road. He greeted him and asked if he was Mike.

"Yes. How ... oh, the others said I was out here. I'm on my way to tell them what I found. It may not be good."

"What?"

"The man we're trying to locate was up there, but the country is impossible. I don't see how he went in there. It's dangerous to a degree that *I* certainly wasn't about to try!"

"Oh. Up above the canyon."

"Above, I could handle. The canyon, I wouldn't even attempt!"

"Maybe he didn't attempt it, either. He might have gone on up the river."

"No. He was after gold. There's a hell of a lot of it, relatively, below the canyon. There's none above, so he wouldn't go on up there. He's savvy about that kind of thing."

They soon parted. Clint went on to his house.

It was the second day later when Tomas came to call out, "Clint! Jantoro!"

He went out on the porch and told him to come on in.

"I am on my way home. Arnaldo asked that I come to tell you that English Dan was found. He was just inside Two Deviltrees Canyon. He is dead."

"Do they know how he died?"

"Yes. There is a hole in his heart."

"A hole?"

"Arnaldo said Nica heard a gun two days ago and went to find him there. He took the body and covered it so the animals won't eat it. He came to Tula today for the supplies and told the council and asked what he should do with the body. It is beginning to stink. Enrique said he would check for the council and they could bury it with a marker for if someone asked where."

"Thanks, Tomas. I'll go up there. Maybe I can find who killed him and why.

"Did you tell the other estrañeros?"

"No. They are not there."

He soon went on the path to his house. Clint told Tyna he was going to see what he could see. Dan was dead. Shot.

"And I said you wouldn't have any of those murders here!"

"Let's hope there's never another one!"

He could take the shorter route from his place and could probably get to the upper canyon ... he wished he'd asked. Dan had seen there was no gold above the canyon and could see it would be next to impossible to go into the canyon from up there. He would go to the lower end and follow the river into the canyon.

That was closer. He also had the point that Nica lived near the lower end, though a gunshot could probably be heard for a number of miles inside the canyon.

He was glad he decided to approach from below when he came to Enrique and Nica just inside the lower end. This was the only easy trail as far as the branch to Nica's place. Nowhere was easy past that point.

They went right and off the trail. It was easy enough to follow where a path was being cut with a machete. Dan had known enough to know how to find the easiest place. Those not knowing nature would assume they could take the smaller scrub a little higher and get through faster. Those in the know took the lower trail. It had more and higher scrub, but it was new growth and easy to cut. The higher was hardened and hard to cut.

Half a kilometer in they came to a tarp that was held in place by stones. They could tell by the smell, as the saying goes, that this was Dan's body.

Clint automatically tore some leaves off a tall weed and crushed them to hold against his nose. The odor was completely cut off.

Dan was shot through the heart. Whoever did it thought no one would find the body for a few days, minimum. The wound didn't hit any bone. It went all the way through, so was probably a high-powered rifle Decomposition and animals would have made it impossible to find how he died after three days without that tarp.

They looked around the area and found a softer spot above some boulders. They dug the grave and buried Dan, then went back down to a little stream, where they took off their clothes and washed them, using the leaves of the tall weed as soap. They also washed themselves, particularly their hair, with the leaves. There was no odor of anything whatever on them or the clothes after fifteen minutes. They put their clothes back on and headed back. Nica took the path to his house and Enrique and Clint went on until the path to Clint's, then Clint went home. They discussed what they would do on the way. Clint asked that Enrique tell no one anything. He would come to town to be there when the gringos returned.

He told Tyna he was going to Tula for the night and would be back tomorrow – hopefully. "So long as they don't know, English Dan has only disappeared. His body won't be found. I want to see how they react to that little detail. They can't take control unless he's legally declared dead."

Tyna grinned and nodded. "So the one who killed him will have to accidentally find his body, which isn't there anymore."

"Yup!"

"Meaning they were better off when he was alive."

"Yup!"

"Mr. Faraday! Did you hear? They found Dan!" Betty called from across the street, just at dusk, in Tula. "He was staying with some people west of here all along!"

!? Surprise! Surprise!

What the hell was going on?

"That's very good news! Is he going back to the business with you?"

"Yes. But not right away. He has a little packet of gold he got from the river. He says he came for gold so he'll get some more before we go back. We can handle a lot of the business from here. We can get a lawyer who can make it all legal, then we won't have to worry for another year, at least. Maybe things will be better by then."

Clint went on with a wave. What was this? He had buried Dan himself.

There was no packet of gold found in his backpack, which should have sent up flags. Clint had the backpack right there in the hostel. He would check it minutely. It had been cursory at the site. No one on the comarca would kill anyone for gold.

Okay. He knew damned well that one or more of that bunch killed him. So they took the gold for someone else to show he was Dan.

He thought. No one knew he had talked with Dan except about philosophy and gold. He carefully went through his memories and was certain he didn't leave them with the impression that he had spent more than a very few minutes with him. Maybe they had someone there who looked enough like him that he wouldn't notice from a distance.

He talked with several people. Enrique said he talked with "that Betty woman" a little and that she had asked him if Clint knew English Dan. He remembered what Clint was doing and said he thinks Clint talked with him for a minute or two one day, but that he hadn't said anything about it.

Clint wondered if they were going to try to use him to establish the imposter's identity. They probably thought he would be like the rest of the Indios. All Englishmen look alike. He grinned to himself.

He went to the cantina for a delicious meal of chicken and rice, frijoles, sweet fried banana and salad. They had guanabana chicha. He would definitely have that!

Halfway through the meal, Betty, Andy, Carl, Mike and (!!) Dan came in. They waved and came over.

"Clint! Hi! You were right. I couldn't make it past that river road, but it didn't matter. There was no gold up that far. It had to come from somewhere inside that canyon and there's no way I would ever try to climb down into that!

"I stayed with the Ramirez family until Mike found me there. I panned a little more gold right outside their door!" He held up the little packet he'd shown Clint before.

This was Dan! What in hell was going on? He was sure that was Dan they buried!

Carl and Andy seemed to be extremely nervous. They probably were worried that Clint would ... but they didn't know Clint knew the other Dan was dead. Mike seemed angry and not a little nervous, himself. They were all too quiet. It wasn't natural for any of them.

Dan's hand was wrapped in a white bandage. "What happened?" Clint asked.

"Oh, this. I was trying to melt the flakes down to make a nugget and burned my thumb and two fingers. I'll get over it! It was plain stupid!"

They chatted awhile, then left.

Okay. This Dan just happened to burn his prints, so they probably wouldn't match the passport. A DNA check would show he wasn't the real Dan. That would be easy to find for anyone as wealthy as he was supposed to be.

Except in one case. Clint grinned. The evil twin wasn't always fiction. This DNA would match. The fingerprints wouldn't.

Something was still 'way off kilter. Why were they so nervous? It had apparently worked.

He thought for awhile, then went to sack out. In the morning, he was going to ... something. He went through the backpack, but there wasn't anything in it that could ... there wasn't anything in it that a prospector would carry!

There was a passport. It was Dan's ... or was it? It was a little too glossy. It was new, and Dan had been a lot of places. This one was stamped for several African countries, Canada, England and here.

Something was set up. It was something very strange. It was something to do with all those businesses. Tomorrow might prove very interesting – for any number of people.

It dawned a beautiful day. A light rain just before dawn had cooled things. The sky was magnificent salmons and golds.

There were six people in the cantina. Clint knew them all and was talking with Liseth about making a garden for the restaurant. Culantro was a weed. Albahaca (basil) was a weed. Oregano was a weed. There were others. They used the spices. It would be easy to plant a patch of each. Albahaca, more than the others, was much better if it was fresh.

Dan came in. There were no bandages on his hand. He waved and came over. He saw Clint staring.

"I said I'd get over it! I didn't burn them as bad as I thought. Carolina put aloe on it and it's only a little red this morning.

"I really like the fried bread here, but I shouldn't eat it. Cholesterol, you know.

"What the hell? I won't live forever, no matter what! What do you call it here?"

"Hojaldres. I love them."

"Okay. I see a lot of questions in your eyes?"

"Who was it we buried up there?"

He laughed. "I knew the minute I walked in the room that something strange was up. You buried someone you thought was me?"

"Yes. They set it up for you to die so they'd get your businesses. There was a body that looked very much like you. He was shot exactly through the heart in a very expert manner. A few days and the animals and decay would make it impossible to say how he died.

"He did look very much like you."

He nodded and looked grim. "Clint, I'm going to

tell you a long and unbelievable tale. I won't blame you if you don't believe it, but hope you'll give me a slight benefit of the doubt.

"It had to look very strange to you that those people would show up here?"

"Very."

"I found out about what they were doing about three months ago. The body was supposed to be me. They did such a good job that no one could tell it wasn't me from twenty feet away.

"I do own a lot of companies. I do run off to hide and have my little adventures.

"I was born into a family that was always big in businesses. We accumulated vast fortunes. It has to do with relatives in the really big world leaders nobody knows much about, the major money manipulators.

"No. Not Rothschilds nor Rodenfelders. I never liked those people I was forced to be around and to deal with on a daily basis since I was fourteen or fifteen years old.

"When I was eighteen, I sneaked away for my first adventure. I went whitewater rafting with a bunch my own age. The thrills were truly unbelievable. I became an adrenalin addict right then and there. I had never been in any danger whatever in my life. I found it felt good!

"They found me and returned me to what I then

knew was a brainwashing technique. It was four years before I found a way to sneak off again. I went skydiving, then on a jungle trek where I had to sign fifty or more papers saying they weren't responsible for anything under any circumstances, anywhere – or whatever! It was something beyond ecstacy. I actually fell in a ramp thing that wasn't secured properly on one end and broke an arm! I wasn't invulnerable! What a rush!

"They found me when I went to the hospital, but I was twenty one, rebellious, and not nearly so easy to order around anymore. It was only a year and two months later that I sneaked away to go to Borneo, to the raw reality of the way we were meant to live. One fellow on the trip died when a snake bit him and we were ten miles from any aid, and that up a swift river. Another almost died when the boat hit a submerged log and he was thrown overboard. There were crocodiles. We barely got him out of the water.

"I would rather die than give that up.

"I had to go back to England, then. My father died. My mother had a breakdown and died three weeks later, not even knowing her own name. I was suddenly fifty one percent owner of something over seventy five million pounds worth of businesses. I had no choice but to try to be a business magnate.

"It didn't work. I sneaked off to Australia and the outback for two years plus. I was in constant danger there because of where we were and what we were doing. I was actually trained for guerilla jungle warfare! Six of my companions were killed when a training truck went off the path and hit a live mine! I was in the following truck.

"Back to Merry Old. I managed to invest in two more businesses that were going belly up. They made a fast comeback with help from my other companies and were soon my top moneymaking holdings. I *am* very good at business. Genetic, I suppose.

"I was getting complaints from my partners, but I was majority. They could kiss my royal ass!

"Next was Africa. All over. It was the first time someone tried to kill me. I had seen a man on the street in M'Kish who was like looking into a mirror. Two people later were talking to me like old friends, though I had never seen them before. They were even calling me by my correct name!

"Then I almost had a fatal accident. A car I had rented and was driving was forced off the road in an inaccessible place. My guerilla training kicked in and I managed not to be at the car when the man who looked exactly like me and someone in those Arabian robes came to look into the car. The one in the robes had a large mallet. I assume he was going to be damned sure I died in that accident!

"I theorized that someone – or someones – were determined the major stockholder was going to die. They would inherit the businesses.

"Then why the look-alike?

"I went back to England and studied everything about the businesses that concerned me in any personal sense. I found that, should I die naturally in England, France, Germany, Canada or the United States, the companies would revert to a holding company secretly owned by an uncle, Robert Westhampton.

"I had met Uncle Bob rather briefly on several occasions when I was quite small. He looked so much like my father I wondered if they were twins. It turned out they were. Father had the business smarts, Bob the woman magnet charm.

"I remembered when Uncle Bob got married to a woman a few years back. There was a big stink because he ran off from a woman who had his son.

"I was suspicious and I have the investigators for the companies in England. I had the son of Bob checked out. It seems his name is Nathaniel Edgar Westhampton. He is within three months of my own age. His picture, taken four years ago, looks like me, twenty pounds lighter.

"The investigator found he had gone into the London branch of my holding company when I was in Borneo. They thought it was me, that I had returned secretly, had lost some weight and was checking up on the company, surreptitiously. He stayed but one day. He even managed to get the woman, who knew me slightly, to hand him some financial records.

"So. There was a scheme afoot to replace me with that first cousin. He has apparently gained enough muscle weight to match my own and had the one noticeable difference, the odd shape of the ears, altered.

"They plan to kill me off somewhere, but not in any of the listed places, where he would inherit automatically. I can't understand why."

"Is Uncle Bob still alive?"

"I don't think so. I sort of remember he died of some kind of cancer or something four or five years ago. I wasn't in England at the time."

"Then I would say he doesn't know the list of countries. He thinks ... that they are using him because he looks like you and they would install him as CEO and he will live very well for the rest of his life.

"It might be a good ... no. He's dead. I have to wonder why!"

"Because someone thought it was me? Why was

he there?"

"He was there in Africa. It gets more involved. I think that, just maybe, some of the plotters are plotting against other of the plotters! I really do!

"We have to come up with some kind of plan to expose them, not to the police, to each other."

"We think much alike on that, too."

Andy and Betty came in and hailed them. Clint invited them over. He said they were just through with their breakfasts, but he could always use another cup of the coffee. He was an addict, and this was grown and dried and ground right there. It was as good as any coffee they would ever taste. Panamá coffee was world famous as among the best.

"We were going to look around this place for a little while before we have to go to Panamá City for the legal stuff," Betty said. "I like the native costumes. I find the people are very friendly and kind."

Dan slightly winked at Clint. "Oh, I've decided that stuff can wait until I get back. After all, the meeting's over and done for the year. It won't make an anthill. Clint says there's a shorter way to the gold – he has friends that know where it is from the bottom end. He can take me close. I did come to find a lode of gold, so I'll stay until I find my lode of gold!"

"No!" Andy cried.

"Oh, why not?" Betty asked. "As he said, the meeting's over for the year. We can call this a vacation. It's been that for me. I haven't relaxed this much in years!"

"Business won't wait for you to take any damned vacation!" Andy spat.

"Sure it will!" Dan said, happily. "How many times have you wailed about me taking a vacation at just the wrong time and blah, blah, blah. For the most part, things went much better without me. They will this time. I know business."

Andy looked like there'd be steam shooting from his ears any second, but he shut up.

They sat in almost silence until Dan said he'd go find some things, then head for the mountains. Clint said he was going home.

About an hour after Clint got home Dan came to call him. He went out front and Dan said he would appreciate it if Clint would show him where the lower path was and where they buried the phony him. He said he had an idea. What if Dan Westhampton were to stumble on the body of – Dan Westhampton!?!

"I ain't about to dig him up," Clint said.

"I know that and you know that. They don't know that!"

"Might work! We can try."

Clint called Tyna and Nito and introduced Dan. He gave Tyna some instructions and he and Dan headed along the path. They were almost to the path to Nica's house when they heard a faint argument between a couple of howler monkeys back the way they had come. Clint grinned

"It seems we're followed. We can really make this thing work, now, but we have to be careful. Whoever it is might be an expert with a high-powered rifle."

"Ah-hah! We can plot as well as the plotters, wouldn't you say?"

"Yes. We'll wait until they're close to discover the body. If it had been dragged out into the sun in the lantana and skinny-stinger weed it would be preserved this long. Animals wouldn't go into it and insects are poisoned by it. It even acts as a mild antibiotic. Decomposition of the surface would be slowed tremendously.

"Buzzards wouldn't be bothered by any of it, but they wouldn't know that. Here's what we'll do!"

"Okay! There he is! It's Mike and ... Carl," Dan whispered. Clint nodded and moved back to near where they'd found the body. He said, in a normal voice, "Dan, don't get any closer. Those plants he's laying in are poisonous. He's a little bloated. I suppose he's been dead for three or four days.

Maybe as much as six. The lantana keeps a lot of insects away and that stinger weed is a natural antibiotic. They both repel animals.

"If you weren't standing right there I'd swear it was you! Do you have a twin?"

"No, but people tell me I have a cousin who looks so much like me that they've embarrassed themselves by going up to him and slapping him on the shoulder or making a crude remark that's a joke among us.

"Clint? What is he doing out in the middle of the jungle in a comarca in Panamá?

"This is strange. Some people said they saw him in Africa, once. I'd had an accident, well, it was no accident. I was forced off the road. I was stunned or something and wandered for some time before I came back to my senses. He was there! Now he's here!

"Clint, am I supposed to be the one laying there in that weed patch?"

"It's damned well more than a wild possibility!"

"That would be why they're here, too. It would be why they're acting so strangely."

"They would end up with the businesses if you kick off?"

"No. I made my holdings part of a continuing company. I saw some terrible things in Africa and Borneo that need attention. I've donated a few million pounds to them. They will become the de facto owners of all of it."

"Do these partners here know that?"

"I think probably they ... don't. I did it just before sneaking off here."

"So. They have an imposter here to die as you. You'll then ... but that doesn't make any sense! You'd still be here!"

"Which means they would use him to set something up, then he'd go. That *is* supposed to be me there.

"Clint, I was supposed to travel along this path into the canyon. I wouldn't come back out. He would come out as me. He ran into one of those Fer de Lance snakes or something and their clever plan went awry."

"I wonder! I'm going to ... give me those yuca sacks. They're nylon and'll keep me on top of the plants. I want to check to see what killed him. A snake would leave him a lot more bloated than that!"

They made some light sounds and said a word or two, then Clint said, "Your snake has about a thirty ought six size fang that's long enough to go right through him!" There was a slight rustling sound a short distance outside of the thick copse of shrub they were staging this in. Clint grinned and called, "Dan, take your pistol and check it.

Have my rifle ready. We might be followed. Nica will be watching. He probably knew about the body and knows who shot him. He wouldn't say anything. He doesn't want the hassle."

"He would leave him there like that?"

"It's nothing, to him. The body will be covered by the vines in another couple of days and he won't decompose fast enough to stink much. If he starts to stink much, the buzzards will find him and finish the job in a day."

"You're going to leave him there?"

"You want to carry that out?"

"No. We'll let whoever shot him think he hasn't been found. We can see who asks all the wrong questions when I get back."

"Sounds like a plan!"

Nica came to the front porch and called. Tyna said Clint was at the stream and pointed. He went there to find Clint playing with Nito in the water. He stripped and joined them.

"Wapping?" Clint asked in the faddish Wadi-Wadi greeting.

"Nothing. I'm going into town and stopped by to tell you that English Dan went into the canyon and the two who were following you came back this way maybe half an hour after. They were not decided if they would go or not to where you and English Dan made your stage, as you call it. I made some noise close and they went back this way very fast.

"You say the Michael man will think I saw him shoot the dead man. I will be most careful in town. They are still there, I think."

"I'll go with you. You can see Mike and not pay any attention to him."

Nica nodded. They swam a few more minutes, then climbed out and laid on the large boulder to dry. Clint took Nito to Tyna and said he was going into Tula with Nica. She said to bring a sack of rice back with him. And some cooking oil.

Nica told Clint about the times people had gone into the canyon to get a little gold to buy things. He had gone in to get the money for a dozen machetes and two pairs of work boots and some beautiful purple pants with a dark green shirt and fancy black shoes for if he ever wanted to dress up for anything. Clint knew the Indios loved colors and could picture Nica, with the body of a Greek god, wearing purple pants and a green shirt with shiny fancy black Italian shoes.

On an impulse, he hugged him. They continued on. As they came into town they met Arnaldo on his way back to his cantina. They walked together and talked about the crazy gringos. They couldn't decide what to do since Dan went off to look for gold again.

Betty and Andy were sitting in the cantina with coffee. Nica and Clint joined them. Clint told them Nica had a house near where Dan went to find his gold. He used some of it whenever he wanted to buy tools or fancy clothes.

"The gold is on his farm?" Andy asked.

"It's comarca land. He has his house near there. Anyone can get the gold when they need it," Clint answered.

"He has a gold mine he can use anytime he wants? They all can? And it just sits there? Don't they know what gold's worth?!" Andy cried.

"It's worth the time it takes to gather a bit when you want things that aren't available to all here," Clint replied. "Dan understands that. He likes the cultural concept. He'll find a ton of the stuff and only take a little for his trophy case.

"They know what it's worth to you. They don't want to be controlled by a greed for things that don't have any meaning. That's the philosophy Dan and I discussed."

"We have to get through to him that we live in a different culture with a different philosophy. That philosophy won't work there!" Andy said. "The businesses suffer when he won't pay them any attention. The fact that he's personally rich doesn't fit into it!"

"The businesses are suffering because the world economy is a total mess. Whether he's there or not doesn't count for dog shit," Clint countered. "For *you* not to be there makes a difference, I suppose. You run them. He only owns them."

Carl and Mike came in and saw Clint and Nica sitting with Andy and Betty. Mike looked like he couldn't believe what he was seeing and like he wanted to make a quick exit. Carl was just very nervous. Clint waved to them. They came over.

"Mike, Carl, this is Nica. He lives up close to the gold mine Dan wants to find.

"So! How are things with you?"

"Er," Mike answered.

"Regular," Carl said. "I don't believe I've met anyone who lives close to a gold mine nobody mines before. Mucho gusto!"

"We get what we want when we need it," Nica said. "I believe I've seen you from a distance in the mountains. Mike, too. It seems that a lot of gringos are wandering around there lately. I can't figure out what they're after. I don't care, so long as they don't bother my cows and chickens or trample my gardens."

"I guess we're all here after the gold, in our own way," Carl said. "We have a different point of view about it. I hear Dan asked the chief if he could get some and was told he could have what he could carry. I wish I had that agreement! I've found a little in the river."

"Did you ask?" Clint asked, amused.

"No. Why?"

"Dan asked."

"And he can take whatever he can carry!" Betty said, happily. "Now, why didn't we think of something so obvious?"

"Your philosophy makes subterfuge and theft priorities in the world," Clint replied. "The obvious, that the council will tell you that you can have what you can carry, never occurs to you. The gold is a thing in nature that the people can use. There've got to be tons of the stuff up there."

"I get a couple of pounds when a lot of us want to go to Soloy to shop," Nica said. "It's too much trouble for some to go into the high mountains. I bring enough for everybody. The man at the exchange gives us maybe a third of what he pays, but it is enough for what we need. We can get all we want."

"You know he's cheating you of two thirds of the price?!" Mike cried.

"It is worth what we decide it is worth. It's what we need. Who cares if he gets a lot more and has to worry that someone is as much a thief as he is and will steal it from him as he steals from us. Nature will even out in life. The thief will often find there are other thieves even more clever and devious than himself. It amuses us."

Clint laughed. "If I had a camera here to get the looks on your faces!"

Betty was the only one there who seemed to be enjoying the conversation. She grinned at Clint and laughed. "So we're silly slaves to gold and money. Clint said it to Dan, who told me about it. We never own the gold. It owns us.

"That's life. I've enjoyed this vacation more than any I can remember, but the persistent call of the unwild is getting louder and louder. I'm ready to go back home to live in the prison of my money."

"Well, we failed in what we came here for. We might as well go. I think Dan will come back today or tomorrow. He can pick up all the gold he can carry in minutes, apparently," Mike said. "I think I'll go meet him."

"I would not advise that you do that," Nica said coldly. Mike looked shocked, but said he was probably right. They didn't know for sure if Dan would get back this month.

He got the point, there! Clint thought.

They chatted a few minutes, then Nica and Clint left. Clint thought it would be interesting to see how Mike explained what Nica said and why he didn't need a reason to agree.

They did their shopping for awhile. Mike came to say he would like to speak with Nica privately. Clint shrugged and said he'd be at the cantina for one more cup of coffee before he started back.

Nica reached into his pocket and pressed the "call" button. It was set to Clint's phone. Clint hit the answer and listened.

"... to know if you ever saw any of us up there before. Maybe two or three days before."

"Yes. I saw you shoot the man."

There was a moment of dead silence. "You didn't report it?"

"To whom? You gringos seem to think what you

do is important to us. It is not. We don't care, but you should not do things like that. Nature will punish you in its own way."

"But ... Dan and Clint found the body. It wasn't where I had ... where he died."

"I placed him in the skinny-stinger weed so he would not stink. I did not have time to bury him."

"Did you tell Clint about it?"

"Why would I? He would not care. Even when he and Dan found the body he did not ask."

"Why would Clint find the body and not report it?"

"I imagine because he is like me. He does not want to have the disruption in his life it would cause. This is not the city. We do not find the same things important."

"But ... the police. He works with them. He would report it to them."

"Why? There are no police here. This is not the city. You are not Indigeno. Had the man been an Indigeno we would have told the council and they would have you chopped with ten machetes and we would bury you in the shame grave."

"That's it? Nobody cares?"

"Why would we? Maybe with English Dan because he has shown he is a friend to us and he has been honest with us."

"You won't tell anyone? Clint won't tell

anyone? It's over?"

"Why would anyone do something that will disrupt his life because of something that is of no concern to him or his people?"

"Faraday is not your people."

"Yes. Clint is declared Ngobe. He lives within our culture and our philosophy."

"Thank you. I call you a friend."

"I am neither friend nor enemy. I am me, you are you. We have met. We will pass on."

"Caio!"

There was silence when the phone was shut off. Clint waited until Nica came. They headed home.

"I think you just made it a lot safer for a lot of people," Clint said. "You saved Dan's life, I suppose. Mike would be out there to kill him."

"English Dan knows jungle warfare. Mike does not."

"You have a point."

Clint turned in at the path to his house. Nica went on. Dan was sitting on the porch with Nito sitting on his lap. Tyna was just bringing them some lemonade. Clint hugged Tyna and sat in the other chair to take Nito.

They sat for a minute, then Dan said, "There's a much richer lode about a kilometer higher. I found a lot in the river above where the people get their gold and climbed on. It's rough country. I got my trophy from the higher one. I can feel I found it. Eureka and all that. The Indios wouldn't bother to look higher because they can get all they want right there. Why make more work for yourself?

"I'm going to leave a couple of pounds of it here for Nito. I took about ten pounds too much to carry all that way and left about eight pounds by Nica's path. I suppose he can use it to buy new clothes or something for the house."

"He'll use it next time a bunch go to Soloy. Maybe he'll get another set of purple and green clothes for himself."

Dan laughed. "If we see some dude dressed like that back home, you immediately think they're gay. Here, the men look like those Italian statues. They wear that stuff and it never crosses your mind. They look good in striking colors."

"Yes. Nobody cares who's gay or not gay here," Tyna said. "Some people are, some are not.

"Clint, I'm going to make some things for Nito with the gold. It is pretty. It will go well with his purple and green clothes!"

They teased a bit. Dan would stay the night. He and Clint would walk into Tula in the morning. Tyna and Nito would go this time. She wanted to see her friends there.

They went to the stream to bathe, ate a delicious dinner of curried pork that Clint prepared, chatted into the night, then slept well, getting up at the sunrise when a dozen roosters began calling to each other. It was a more subtle dawn than usual, with only a little gold and pink tinting on the few high fleecy clouds. They were in good spirits as they walked leisurely along the path. Dan's backpack weighed about eighty pounds, but he was used to it and refused to let Clint carry any of it. It was his trophy and he was going to deliver it, himself!

"I really love these people and this life, but I would go crazy in another month. I cannot and will not lay around. It's what I'm running from with these little excursions. This is a much more seductive place that calls for that life.

"I envy your ability to phase this easy life into interesting ways to spend much of your time. Tyna showed me the garden she has there. I think you enjoy a much more varied diet than I do. You have the chickens and a cow for milk and a sow who has eight pigs Tyna says you will give to people, except the one. You have bananas and coconuts and pineapples and those cashew fruits and breadfruit and those guanabana things that are delicious and water apples and pears and limes and who knows what else for the picking.

"I wish I were the farming type. You are living in a true paradise. I don't know if it's not enough for me or merely too much. I have the genetic greed and business thing, I suppose. I couldn't well be happy here. It is a sad lacking in me.

"Different people have different needs inside," Tyana said. "What we need is here. What you need is only partly here."

"Are all you Indios so intelligent and so deeply philosophical?"

"Yup!" Clint replied, with a laugh. They chatted until they were in Tula. Tyna went to visit her cousins while Dan and Clint went to the hostel. Betty was sitting on the front porch and greeted them. Andy and Carl heard them come in and came out on the porch. Carl asked, "Well, Daniel.

Did you find your gold mine?" as several people came to welcome Clint and Dan.

"Yes. I have my trophy." He opened the heavy backpack and dumped the large lumps of gold onto the floor. Eighty pounds of pure gold.

"Jesus H. Christ! Don't show everyone and his dogs what you have!" Andy cried.

"Why not? They don't care," Dan replied. "I left some of it by the path for Nica and gave some to Nito. This will be enough for my trophy case. I actually found another lode that's more than the one the people are using."

"That's got to be a hundred or more pounds of pure gold! That's twelve hundred ounces! That's a million pounds worth right there! You just dump it on the floor in front of who knows who!?"

Betty laughed. "They can go up there and get all they want. Why would they care? What's there is community property. The chief said I can go take what I can carry if I want. Seeing that, I'm seriously thinking about it!"

"You'd die from exertion before you even got there," Dan said. "It wore me into exhaustion, but the return was a lot easier. I had cut the path on the way in.

"I want a long shower, then we can head back to Soloy and Merry Old tomorrow – or I can.

"I just thought of something! I can take this from

here, but they aren't going to allow me to take it anywhere once I'm outside the comarca!"

"I'll have a couple of friends in Soloy carry it to Panamá City in yuca sacks. I have friends who'll get it sent to London as cheap deck freight," Clint suggested. "If it's deck freight, it doesn't have much value. We can put it in something heavy and no one will even glance at it twice."

"I'll have it taken to the Panamanian Embassy in London as furnishing for the place. You can pick it up whenever you want," Generoso, a chief counselor, said. "They can't question that by their own law."

"I can't even pay you for that!" Dan cried. "You can get all the gold you want!"

"You will have to pay for the airplane to take it to London and for the service to deliver it to the embassy," Generoso replied. "Now. What are we going to do about this Michael character with you? He became very sorely drunk last night and assaulted a man. We would allow the man to handle it except that he was trying to take the man's daughter away from the refrescos and the man tried to stop him. The girl ran away and has made a charge. We have to deal with it because the comarca law says that people may not assault one another without just cause. Natio had that cause. Michael did not. It is also against comarca law to place your hands on a woman who objects."

"He tried to rape a girl?" Dan asked. "How old is she?"

"I believe perhaps fourteen or fifteen years," Generoso replied.

"He tried to molest a *child*!?" Betty demanded, shocked.

"No. A young girl," Clint answered. "She's of legal age at twelve here. That figures into it only to the degree it outrages the council."

"Where is he?" Dan asked.

"He is detained in his room here," Generoso said. "If you are leaving, we will not pursue it, but he may never return to the comarca. If he comes back, he will be executed."

"Execution is what he deserves!" Betty said, acidly. "I never trusted him much. If he tried to force himself onto a child, he should be stood against the wall and shot squarely between the eyes! The very idea!"

"We just chop them up with machetes here," Generoso replied.

"Better yet!" she shot back "I never understood why he was so insistent that we try to find Dan. It's not like it was the first time he was away at the meetings. He's away more than he's there!

"Carl and he were the only ones who thought it

was important. I wonder why more than ever, now!"

"I suppose he and Carl wanted to find me out in the jungle somewhere and knock me over to get the companies," Dan said, casually. "It wouldn't be the first time he tried that. It was the plan in Africa, but I'm not so stupid as they believed. I've been ahead of them ever since I found out about Nathaniel. Had he conducted himself in a civilized manner I would have allowed him to return to his home to lick his wounds. With this, I will not! If it's just me, it amuses me. When he assaults children it becomes something else.

"Carl, you and Mike were observed when you followed Clint and myself when we discovered Nathaniel's body. It became very clear what you were up to, then. It made my life more interesting to know you plotted to kill me off. I don't know why Mike killed Nathaniel. He was part of the original plan to substitute him for me. I knew it was part of a plan of some kind since Africa, where I first encountered him.

"Generoso, you will find the body of a man, Nathaniel Edgar Westhampton, in the mountains just beyond the path to Nica's house. He was shot through the heart. Mike was observed (Clint very slightly shook his head) carrying a rifle, not far from the place at about that same time by some children working in a vegetable garden.

"There are no rifles here except his. He will have it in his room. Be most careful!"

"I see," Generoso replied. "We discovered the rifle when we consigned him to the room and have removed it. He will be dealt with severely by comarca law for more than one infraction.

"You say this Carl person here was involved with him?"

"They were observed with him and with the murdered man, Nathaniel Westhampton, on more than one other occasion," Clint said.

"My dear god! That was what it was, was what it had to be!" Betty suddenly exclaimed.

"What?" from Dan.

"I saw you in the town last week and you said you had to hide right away and that I was not to tell anyone I had seen you. You would explain later, but to go along with saying I was here to look for you! You acted most strange and didn't remember talking with me before coming on this trip! It was most strange!

"It was *him*, not you!"

"If you saw someone here before I came from my friend's place, it was not me."

"So. Why was he shot, Carl?" Clint asked.

"I don't even know what the hell you're talking about! I'm not saying a thing without benefit of counsel!"

"I am a counselor, though I know that is not your meaning," Generoso said. "This is the comarca. We do not have a lot of technicalities and lawyers here. I am the judge and jury. I base my decisions upon the evidence provided. The evidence is not so strong against you, but your refusal to answer our questions is noted.

"There is no comarca law against plotting a murder. There is a law against accomplishing that murder. My understanding is that you planned to kill Dan. He is alive. You did not accomplish that and have broken no serious law.

"We have a slight complication in that someone did get killed. It is only to determine if you were part of that and what part. The evidence that the man was murdered directly by this Mike person is overwhelming.

"You can tell me about the entire thing or I will be forced by the situation to believe you were part of that murder.

"This is serious. Like Panamanian law, you are guilty until you prove you are not here."

Carl looked around, not finding a sympathetic eye in the place.

"Well?" Betty demanded.

"I had nothing to do with killing Edgar. We called him that, not Nathaniel."

"That won't do at all!" Generoso warned. "You would say that without regard to the facts."

"Start with when you got drawn in until now," Clint suggested. "It can't hurt you. I know the law."

He sighed heavily and started: "I was attending a meeting between myself and Mike and Dan in Sydney about four years ago. We discussed some things when it suddenly dawned on me that I was not believing what was happening. You turned to look toward Mike and your ears were larger and misshapen on the lobe.

"I asked what was going on and said this was not Dan Westhampton. He looked like a twin, but the ears were different.

"Mike introduced Edgar. He said he always had the feeling that the two were identical, but not the same person. He didn't know why. I had seen the problem! The ears were different!

"We made a plan to wait until you were on one of these trips and substitute him for you long enough to get a few legal papers reassigned by him. We had the recordings of your voice and your use of certain phrases. We had pictures of your idiosyncracies. It couldn't fail! Even a DNA comparison would prove inconclusive because your fathers were twins!

"There was never a plan on my part to harm you

in any way – other than financial. You would still have some millions of pounds, no matter what.

"Mike and Edgar followed you to Africa. I learned that they had tried to kill you there and became wary. I demanded that this would end at that moment, should that be any least part of the plan. I made it plain that I knew of the list of countries where Edgar would receive nothing and made it as plain that we would use only places that were *not* on that list!

"You then came here. Mike said, for the plan to work, we would have to have a majority of stockholders present. He contacted Andy and Betty and gave them a story about the terrible economy and that we had to find you and get you to assign voting rights for when he was away.

"Betty said it would be a vacation, that she had heard Panamá was a paradise, so why not? Andy said anything to get a control where you wouldn't ignore the business to our disadvantage.

"We came here to find you where people knew you were. I did not know that Mike planned to kill you and substitute Edgar permanently.

"Mike learned you were in the mountains and about where. He said he would return from the mountains with Edgar, we would convince him to give us majority voting through a small percent proxy to each of us, meaning we would have little more ability than at that time.

"Mike told me about the rest of the mess after it happened.

"Mike went to the upper valley. He found that you knew of a lower path to get into the valley. There was no gold in the river above so the lode is in that valley.

"He had left Edgar below. He would wait until you entered the valley, knowing you would not return for a minimum of two days, which would be plenty of time for our plan.

"He went to the lower path and saw the person he thought was you going into the valley. You were cutting a path through. He found you and shot you. It would be perfect!

"He went to where Edgar was supposed to be waiting. Some children had told Edgar it was easy to get to the gold by cutting a rather short path through some scrub for about two hundred meters, then following the stream up to the gold lode. He apparently decided he would get to the gold first.

"Mike shot our plant. He learned that you were at some friend's place for a few days before you went back to find the lode. You know the rest."

"So. We never could figure why Edgar was killed. It was because Mike thought he was shooting me. We couldn't think of reason anyone would kill him," Dan said.

"It would seem so," Generoso replied. "Bring Mike here."

Two of the nearby men went to the room and came back with Mike between them. He was protesting and saying they couldn't treat him this way! He would have his lawyers bring a world court suit against them.

"Sit down and shut up!" Clint snarled. "You're being given special treatment as it is. If you were one of our people, we'd have already buried you."

"I demand the right to speak with the Canadian Embassy!"

"There is no Canadian or other embassy here on the comarca," Generoso replied. "You are charged with forcing yourself on a woman and assaulting her father. A secondary charge is the murder of a man called Edgar Something. You may make claim as to the falsity of the charges, but with proof, not mere words."

"I don't have to prove anything!"

"Yes, you do. Am I to understand that you have no refutation to offer?"

"I don't even know what you're talking about! I never forced myself on any woman and I never assaulted any woman's father and I certainly didn't murder anyone!"

"Four people state you placed your hands on Gisele Romero, that her father defended her against you and that you assaulted him."

"Okay. I was depressed by a business failure and got a little drunk. I may have grabbed at some bar whore, but I didn't assault anyone! I only defended myself when *he* attacked *me*!"

"*Whore*?!" Betty screeched. "She's fourteen years old!"

"Please do not interrupt," Generoso said, sternly. "If she was fourteen or forty makes no difference. That she was in a refresqueria, not a bar, means she may not be called a prostitute. That the man he claims has assaulted him is the father of the woman is important here. He has a right to defend his family in whatever way he can.

"You are determined to have, in truth, assaulted the father of a woman who was defending her from an assault, by you, upon her.

"The murder charge is also determined to be truth.

"Is there anything further?"

"What does that mean?" Mike asked.

"Clint, perhaps you will tell him what it means? I will correct you if you don't have a clear understanding."

"The way I understand it is that the father has the right to exact justice in a degree that does not exceed the charges. In short, I hope he takes you out in the field and beats holy living hell out of you.

"The murder, I don't know."

"The victim has no family here?" Generoso asked.

"I am a cousin and I am the one he meant to kill," Dan said.

"I see. It can be very unpleasant for a man to not succeed in such a case. You have the right to exact justice in any way you see fit. I would suggest that you kill him, but realize that is not the way your law works, which is why there are so very many who flaunt that law.

"You may state your desires in the matter."

"May I suggest that you allow him to leave and return to Canada?" Dan said. "If you will give a written judgement that states that he has killed someone here, that it is proven in court, and that he may not come here again for any reason it will suffice. He will, of course, be stripped of any interests in any business he may be engaged in with any person here today. That will handle it.

"You have demonstrated that you know how these greedy people depend on their business connections. He will be left with very little, for all his plots and plans."

"Very well. It seems too little, but I do not know the psychology of your people.

"Sr. Romero, what is your decision regarding

your daughter?"

"I think my friend, Clint, and his friend, Dan, have done enough for justice. He didn't succeed with my daughter and he didn't do anything to me that is lasting. He hit me, I hit him.

"I would make it stronger that if he comes back here I may kill him at will."

"Done. I think the woman on the TV always says 'Caso cerrado!' That is what I say.

"Sr. Mike, you will be off of the comarca within twenty four hours or any person who is here legally may solve the problem as they see fit. You are declared outlaw as of that time."

Everyone went their own way. Betty couldn't believe they would let a man who was convicted of murder walk around the streets. Clint said he would get out of the comarca at his own expense, that way.

"How far is Soloy?" Dan asked.

"The helicopter brought us," Betty said. "We can call and he can be out in about two hours."

Dan laughed. "Ah! *We* can be out in about two hours. He has to pay two hundred dollars for the trip. I wonder, does he have two hundred dollars left?"

"I have a lot more than two hundred dollars," Mike replied. "I'll be gone. You might not find it so easy to throw me out of the business. I don't think Canada will follow the decision of some judge on a reservation."

"I think that perhaps you fail to take into consideration that I own fifty one percent of that company," Dan said, easily. "Betty owns her percent, Andy owns his percent. Carl doesn't matter. He may sell his percent to us or we can vote him out. He's plotted to a fraudulent practice to gain control, thus is not fit to hold voting stock.

"I think I'll want to spend the time until the chopper gets here with my new friends. I hope to return here at times.

"Clint, Tyna, I wish you the very best in all things and for all time."

They chatted for a few more minutes. Clint said goodbye to Betty and Dan. He nodded to Andy, then he and his family went home.

<u>*An E-mail*</u>

Dearest friends – I have been here in London for but four months and find myself wanting to find another adventure. I have given my voting rights by proxy to Betty, who has the level head among the group. Carl and Mike have formed a partnership and plan to found a brokerage business in Mexico. I have investigated and find it is not what they believe it to be. I find this is proof enough that Carl was with Mike in the plot to knock me off and take the business. I will not inform them about the plans by some people who are much the same as they to divest them of whatever they have. Carl has sold his stock to Andy and Betty for market value. I am allowing Mike to hold his stock as non-voting. Should he wish to sell, I am not interested.

I am planning another adventure in your part of the world. I find there is little in this part to interest me. It is a thing in Brazil and Argentina. I will be a sort of independent soldier of fortune. I will greatly enjoy the danger. This will be a more imminent and direct danger than I have known before.

I wish you well. I wish Nito well and I wish Tyna well. If this were Merry Old with you, I would place a fund to ensure that Nito has the very best education. Oxford, don't you know. He will know more than could be taught there of life before he reaches the age where he would attend. I know he would not like to leave paradise for the impersonal extreme sordidity of cities.

My trophy case is almost filled. I have tried to be realistic about things. I have enjoyed more and better experience than almost anyone. I want to see it filled, if I live to be of an age to sit back with a fine Scots whiskey and cigar (which is bullshit. I don't like cigars) and reminisce about the time when.... You would be a major part of that excursion down memory trail. I hope I am some part of your fond memories when you reach that time of life.

Well, off to the races, eh what?

All my love – Dan

"That was nice of him," Tyna said, reading the e-mail. "I think he's crazy, but it's a good crazy."

"He's alright. He was just born into the wrong family at the wrong time. The late eighteens or the early nineteen hundreds, he would be away on safari or something ... not really. Without the money he couldn't do the things he wants to do."

"Without our money we would be doing exactly

what we're doing. We have the best life."

Clint smiled. Nito came in carrying the solid gold carved horse Generoso had made for him. Generoso was one of the few people who could carve gold with such amazing fine detail. The horse weighed more than three pounds. Forty thousand dollars worth of gold and a million dollars worth of art. He put it carefully onto the little table. He knew pure gold was soft, so he shouldn't drop it or bang it around.

Clint took the computer qwerty board to reply to Dan's e-mail: *Dan – Friend, we all wish you the best. Nica and Enrique send greetings. We hope you find the adventure that makes you want to find another. I would hate to think you would stop seeking. I would hate it if I did. All our love – Faraday Family*

He laid back. All in all, he was the luckiest man alive.

C. D. Moulton's works are available on most major outlets as printed or e-books. CD writes the CD Grimes, PI, mysteries, the Det. Lt. Nick Storie mysteries, the Clint Faraday mysteries, the Flight of the Maita science fiction series, books on orchid culture and many others of many types. Mystery, adventure, intrigue, science fiction, humor, fantasy, paranormal, mild erotica, and factual.

www.ingramcontent.com/pod-product-compliance
Lightning Source LLC
Chambersburg PA
CBHW061631130726
47996CB00003B/1223